Haunted Treasure!

*Look out for more stories
about this spooky family!*

Head for Trouble!

Haunted Treasure!

Frank Rodgers

SCHOLASTIC

Scholastic Children's Books,
Commonwealth House, 1-19 New Oxford Street,
London, WC1A 1NU, UK
a division of Scholastic Ltd
London ~ New York ~ Toronto ~ Sydney ~ Auckland
Mexico City ~ New Delhi ~ Hong Kong

First published by Scholastic Ltd, 2002

Text and illustrations copyright © Frank Rodgers, 2002

ISBN 0 439 98234 0

Printed and bound by Cox and Wyman Ltd, Reading, Berks

2 4 6 8 10 9 7 5 3 1

Chapter One

The Ghost Train Chills were the strangest, most unusual relatives anyone ever had. Charlie's Aunt Jill was a vampire, his Great Grandpa McGill a skeleton, his Cousin Bogle a troll and his Uncle Thothage a mummy. They all lived and worked in the Ghost Train at the old funfair on the edge of town, not far from Charlie's house.

Charlie's parents regarded them as a complete embarrasment and even tried to pretend they didn't exist. Whenever they referred to them, which wasn't often, they called them the family's dreadful secret. But Charlie loved the Chills and, grudgingly, his parents allowed him to visit them whenever he wanted.

"So what would you like to do before you go home, Charlie?" asked his aunt that afternoon, her white fangs gleaming. "Shall we play a game? How about Hide and Shriek?"

"Or we could have a little sing-song," suggested McGill, his head bouncing up and down on his bony shoulders.  "I'll play my accordion and Jill can sing. She's got an incredibly beautiful and loud voice, Charlie."

"Er ... I know, Great Grandpa," said Charlie, wincing at the memory. The last time he heard his aunt sing two hundred people had rushed from the school hall. "But..." he went on quickly, "if you don't mind I'd like to do a bit of homework."

"Homework?" cried all the Chills in surprise.

"Whatever for, Charlie?" asked big Bogle, puzzled. "Doesn't it hurt your brain?"

Thothage stirred in his chair and murmured, "Homework's too tiring," before dozing off again.

Charlie looked at his uncle fondly. Everything was too tiring for Thothage. He'd been out of his tomb for over a hundred years and was always trying to catch up on lost sleep.

"You can all help with this homework," said Charlie, pulling an exercise book out of his schoolbag. "We're doing a project on family trees."

"Is that a kind of tree that families can live in, Charlie?" asked Bogle.

"No!" snorted McGill. "A family tree is a kind of plan of your family's history ... who was born when, and all that kind of stuff. Isn't that right, Charlie?"

Charlie nodded. "That's right, Great Grandpa." He smiled at his relatives. "And I need you all to tell me how you fit into my family tree."

"Well," said Jill, patting her towering purple hairdo and smiling at Charlie. "We're all from your father's side of the family, of course. His great  great great grandfather married my great great great grandmother and they lived in a castle in Transylvania. I came here about a hundred years ago, not long after the funfair was built. The Ghost Train was left to me by my Uncle Bill." She pointed to a faded black and white framed photograph of a grinning, bald man on the cobwebby dresser. "That's him."

"He looks very cheery," remarked Charlie, smiling.

"I never met him, but my mother told me he was always laughing," replied Jill.

Charlie made some notes in his jotter. "So really you're my distant aunt, Aunt Jill?"

His aunt grinned and nodded. "We're all a bit distant, Charlie, but we're still your relatives!"

"I'm your father's grandfather," said McGill. "Thothage is an ancestor of your father's, too, and Bogle is related to your great great grandfather's brother."

Charlie frowned down at his jotter. "Er, I think I might have to disguise the names a bit," he said. "If people find out two of my relatives are called Bogle and Thothage they might start asking questions."

"Fair enough, Charlie," replied McGill. "But don't worry if it's all a bit confusing. I'll write it all down for you."

"And what we don't know you can find out at the library, Charlie," said his aunt.

"I'll go tomorrow," replied Charlie. "The library was closed today."

"Closed?" said Aunt Jill. "Why? It's never closed on a Thursday."

Charlie shook his head and frowned. "The old library's falling apart and the council say they can't afford to fix it. The outside badly needs repairing and the inside..." He stopped and made a face.

"What?" asked his aunt.

"Well," Charlie went on, "it's strange but the library's had a lot of bad luck recently."

"What kind of bad luck?" asked McGill.

"A month ago it was a burst pipe that ruined a lot of books," replied Charlie. "Then three weeks ago it was collapsing shelves, two weeks ago broken furniture and this week falling plaster. The librarian reported it to the council but they say it's because the library's so old and run down. They say they might have to close it for good if it goes on like this. Our school has just started a 'Save the Library' campaign."

McGill cracked his bony knuckles. "Every week," he murmured thoughtfully. "Seems a bit regular." He peered at Charlie from under his bushy orange eyebrows. "Do you think the damage might be deliberate?"

"You mean … vandalism?" said Charlie.

"No," replied his great grandfather slowly. "Something sneakier than that."

"Sabotage!" cried Jill.

"Exactly!" replied McGill, his head wobbling excitedly.

"But who would want to sabotage the library?" asked Charlie.

"Someone who doesn't like reading?" suggested Bogle.

"Of course not, you daft troll!" snapped McGill. "Someone who wants to get his hands on the building…"

"Ah!" Bogle interrupted eagerly. "You mean someone who *does* like reading!"

McGill rolled his eyes in exasperation. "No!" he cried testily. "Someone who wants to get his hands on the building so he can tear it down, build a brand new one and charge a fortune for it."

Charlie nodded. "I think people like that are called speculators."

Thothage yawned and opened one eye. "How can we find out if that's true?" he asked sleepily.

"We'll stake out the library this week!" said McGill with relish. "Starting tonight. Oh, I love being a detective!"

Charlie groaned. "But the last time you went out of the Ghost Train you lost your head Great Grandpa," he said. "It took us ages to find it!"

"This time I'll stick it on wi' super-glue!" said McGill. He looked eagerly at the others. "Are you with me?"

"Yes!" cried the other Chills.

"Me too!" said Charlie quickly. "I want to go as well." *To keep an eye on all of you,* he thought.

"Your mum and dad wouldn't hear of it!" cried Jill. "You running around town at midnight with us? Your parents would go into orbit if they found out." She looked at Charlie severely for a moment, then winked. "But don't worry. The library is only just behind the Ghost Train and you'll be perfectly safe with Bogle. He'll pick you up at midnight." She turned and grinned at the big troll. "Won't you, Bogle?"

Bogle beamed.

"Glad to!" he said, flexing the muscles on his huge arms. "I'll not only pick you  up, Charlie ... I'll give you a lift too!"

Charlie laughed. "You made a joke, Bogle."

The big troll scratched his shaggy head. "Did I?" he said. "I didn't know I could be funny."

Charlie grinned. "See you at midnight, Bogle!"

Chapter Two

Brat Gripewater leaned back in the driving seat and smirked.

"This is too easy," he said, looking across the dark, empty street towards the old, crumbling library. "Too easy." He turned and winked at his two cronies, Lance Boyle and Slinky Eels. "Wouldn't you say, lads?"

"Yeah," agreed Lance, grinning from ear to ear. "Their alarm is so old it's practically a museum piece. It's a doddle to turn off each time. The whole operation is dead easy."

"Super dead easy," added Slinky with a snigger. "And nobody has a clue who to blame for all the problems in there. They think it's all accidental. The library will have to close soon. They can't afford to repair everything and keep it open."

Brat smirked again in satisfaction and sighed. "Ah yes," he murmured. "I love it when I'm plotting and planning. As soon as the library closes I'll offer to buy it from the council. Then when it's mine I'll knock it down and build a block of flats. The library's on a main street ... prime location. I'll make a fortune. You have to speculate to accumulate, as they say!"

"You're smart, boss," said Lance, toadyingly. "No wonder you're a millionaire."

Brat chuckled and looked at his watch. "A quarter to midnight," he said. "Off you go. I'll come back for you in an hour once you've..." he grinned nastily and tapped the side of his nose, "improved the interior of the library once again."

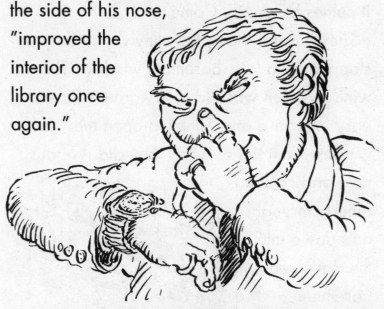

Lance and Slinky grinned too and slipped out of the car. Swiftly they crossed the empty street and went into a narrow alleyway by the side of the library. On the wall just above head-height was the alarm box, its red light winking. Lance took an alarm deactivator from his pocket, pointed it at the box and pressed a button. Immediately the alarm light went out.

"That's the alarm off," he whispered, winking at Slinky. "Gives us an hour before it comes on again. Come on."

They hurried along the alleyway and stopped by a low, basement window. The window-catch was old and worn and it was easy for Lance and Slinky to open the window from the outside. They did it again now and climbed quickly through and down into the darkened basement.

Switching on their torches they threaded their way between the heavy old storage cupboards and bookcases.

"We'll go upstairs later and I'll loosen a few more shelf screws and sabotage a few more chairs," whispered Slinky.

"And I'll do a bit of damage to the computer," hissed Lance. "But before that I think a bit of wrecking is in order down here, don't you?"

Slinky grinned evilly.

"Sure do," he said.

Chapter Three

It was just after midnight and Jill, McGill and Thothage were waiting for Bogle and Charlie in front of the darkened library. Thothage leaned against the railings, eyes closed, trying to have forty winks, but Jill and McGill were wide awake.

"At least you didn't have far to come," whispered Charlie's aunt, when she saw Charlie riding on Bogle's shoulders.

"Let's circle the place first," suggested McGill as Charlie slid to the ground. "That way we can pick the best places to post lookouts." He patted Thothage on the shoulder and a little cloud of dust puffed out.

"What? Who?" Thothage mumbled, startled.

"Wake up, Thothage laddie," muttered McGill. "Rub the sand out of your eyes. It's time for action." He and the others set off down the alleyway at the side of the library.

Yawning, Thothage sleepily pushed himself away from the railings and followed them.

In the basement Lance and Slinky were thoroughly enjoying themselves. They had loosened shelf screws, pulled out wires and cracked the ceiling plaster. Now they were levering off a bit of the old panelling at the back of the basement.

Lance grunted as he pulled heavily on the crowbar. With a soft tearing sound, a big section of the aged wooden panelling gave way and slowly fell off the wall.

"Careful," said Slinky with a snigger as he caught the panelling and laid it on the floor. "You were only supposed to loosen it."

"Who cares," sneered Lance. "They'll think it just fell off the wall because the wood was rotten." He played his torch over the broken plaster behind the panelling. A lot of the plaster had fallen away too, exposing the old stonework underneath. "What's this?" he muttered and peered more closely at the narrow space between two large pieces of crumbling masonry. "There's something there." Cautiously he poked his thumb and forefinger into the gap and withdrew a folded piece of parchment, yellow with age.

Slinky shone his torch on the parchment as Lance carefully unfolded it.

"It ... it's some kind of map," breathed Slinky.

"The boss will want to see this!" muttered Lance.

At that moment a loud clanging sound in the alley made them jump with fright.

"What was that?" yelped Slinky, looking nervously up at the window.

"Don't know!" gasped Lance. "But I think there's somebody up there. Come on, we'll have to find another way out!" He pulled out a mobile phone as he ran for the door. "I'll phone the boss!"

In the alley Bogle picked himself up and righted the dustbins he had knocked over.

"Clumsy," he muttered, looking crestfallen at the others. "Sorry."

26

"You're a silly big ham-footed troll, that's what ye are!" hissed McGill in exasperation. "I saw lights in the basement a moment ago and now they've gone out. Whoever was in there has heard us and scarpered."

"Let's split up," said Jill urgently. "Spread out round the library. One of us is bound to see where they come out!"

"Good idea!" cried Charlie.

Everyone turned in different directions, got entangled with each other, then tripped over Thothage who was having a quick nap on the ground. Down they all went in a jumbled heap and Bogle knocked over the dustbins again.

As they untangled their arms and legs and
sorted themselves out they heard the roar
of a car engine and a screech of brakes,
followed by the sound of car doors slamming.

"Where did that come from?" cried McGill,
still on his hands and knees. He looked
round frantically.

"From over there!" said Bogle, eager to
help. He swung his big arm up and pointed.
"From the front of the library."

McGill stood up just as Bogle threw his
arm out to point.

Thump! The big arm connected heavily
with McGill's head, knocking it clean off
his shoulders.

McGill's head sailed
down the alley like
a football,
bounced
once and
rolled into
the street.

At the same moment there was another roar from the car and it shot across the end of the alleyway ... straight at McGill's head.

Charlie and the Chills caught their breath in horror as the head disappeared beneath the car ... then everyone breathed again as they saw it roll between the wheels and out the other side.

As the car sped away Jill took the headless McGill by the hand and they all dashed down the alleyway into the street. Charlie bent down and looked at the skull anxiously, then smiled with relief as it winked at him.

"Thank goodness you're all right!" he cried. Bogle picked up McGill's head and stuck it back on to his shoulders.

"That's better," said McGill. "I always seem to be losing my head."

"You forgot to use super-glue again, Great Grandpa," said Charlie.

"Just as well, laddie," replied McGill with a grin. "You see, if my head hadn't gone for a wee run we would never have known who was in the car. And it's all thanks to big strong Bogle here for using his arm like a baseball bat."

Bogle blushed with pleasure and Charlie and the others waited expectantly.

"So who was in the car?" asked Charlie. His great grandpa frowned.

"Someone I should have suspected right from the beginning, Charlie," he said grimly.

Charlie stared at him. "Not Brat Gripewater!" he exclaimed.

"It certainly was," replied McGill. "Him and his two cronies!"

"Hah! I might have known!" cried Jill. "He'll stop at nothing to get his hands on property in this town. He even tried to swindle me out of the Ghost Train once!"

"Yes," said McGill. "I had a funny feeling that he'd be involved somehow!"

Chapter Four

Brat looked up from the map spread out on his desk. His eyes were shining with greed.

"What is it, boss?" asked Slinky eagerly, peering over Brat's shoulder at the old parchment.

"Is it something good?" asked Lance.

Brat nodded slowly and looked down again.

"Oh yes," he murmured, a wide grin stretching across his big mouth. "Oh yes!" He pointed to a faint red spot on the map surrounded by tiny writing. "It says there's treasure hidden here!"

Lance and Slinky gasped, their eyes opening wide with excitement.

"Treasure!"

"Yeah, treasure," Brat peered closely at the map

again, and went on, "and by the looks of it, it's right underneath the library."

Lance frowned in puzzlement. "That's a weird place to hide treasure – under a library!"

Brat shook his head and grinned. "It wasn't always a library, Lancey boy." He traced his finger round the outline of a building on the map. "It used to be a castle. The library was built on top of the castle's foundations. The treasure is hidden in the old cellars that run deep under the library basement."

"I see," said Lance, understanding dawning on his face. "So all we have to do is find the old cellars and snatch the treasure?"

Brat frowned and stuck out his bottom lip.

"It's not as easy as that," he said. "I've seen the plans of the library and there's no mention of any cellars. They must have been sealed off when the library was built. So we can't reach the treasure from the library. But..." he went on slowly, his finger following a line on the map, "according to the map the treasure can be reached by following a passageway which starts ... here!" He jabbed his finger at the map.

Then opening a book beside him he checked the spot's location against a modern map of the area. He drew in his breath sharply. "A slight problem," he said in annoyance.

"What, boss?" asked Lance. "Where does the tunnel start?"

Brat looked at his two henchmen through narrowed eyes. "The tunnel entrance is under the Ghost Train," he said.

"What? But why does it start there?" Slinky enquired in confusion.

"Because," Brat said, trying to control his rising anger, "it seems that the land on which the Ghost Train is built used to be part of the castle too. "Not only that," he said, pointing to some writing at the bottom of the map, "it appears that the castle belonged to a family called the Chylles."

"Not ... the Chills who own the Ghost Train?" gasped Lance, aghast.

"Looks like it," snarled Brat angrily.

"But ... but that might mean..." stuttered Slinky.

"Yeah," continued Lance, "that might mean that the treasure belongs to the Chills!"

They looked at Brat in dismay, but Brat just smiled nastily.

"It might," he said. "But what they don't know won't hurt them, will it?" He smirked. "I have the map. They don't know it exists. They probably don't even know about the old castle, never mind that it used to belong to them. Or that there's treasure down there. So there's no problem." Brat smiled in satisfaction and nodded at Lance and Slinky. "Tomorrow night you two will break into the Ghost Train and find the passageway. Then all you have to do is take a little walk along it and nab the treasure. Easy!"

"I ... I don't like Ghost Trains much, boss," stuttered Slinky. "They're scary."

Brat scowled at his quivering henchman.

"Don't be so childish, Slinky," he snapped. "There's nothing to be scared of. It's all fake, you know.
There's nothing
real in the
Ghost
Train."

"I don't know," muttered Slinky. "We were with you that time you tried to diddle the owner and I have to say those Chills looked real to me!"

"It's make-up," replied Brat, annoyed. "Only make-up. Pull yourself together, Slinky."

Lance patted Slinky on the shoulder.

"Don't worry, Slink," he said cockily. "You'll be with me so it'll be all right. Lance Boyle is afraid of nothing!"

"Yes," purred Brat soothingly. "Don't worry. And you know what? If you can't find a way into the cellars from the Ghost Train it's not the end of the world. I'll wait until I buy the library. Then all we have to do is go down to the basement and dig!"

Chapter Five

The Ghost Train Chills spent the next day thinking about Brat Gripewater.

"I don't believe he or his men will go back to the library for a wee while now that they've been disturbed in the act," said McGill. "So at least we've got some breathing space to decide what to do."

"Go to the police?" suggested Bogle.

Jill shook her head. "We've got no proof," she said. "We didn't see them in the library, just driving away from it. There's no crime in that."

Thothage yawned. "I think we should sleep on it," he murmured and laid his head on the kitchen table. He closed his eyes and was just drifting off when a piercing scream tore round the kitchen.

AIEEEE!

"Wh-what?" he mumbled, sitting up. "Were you singing, Jill?"

"No, Thothage," replied Jill, grinning. "It was just the doorbell." She opened the door and Charlie came in.

"Hello, everyone," he said, holding up a big book. "I've just been to the library."

"How is the old library?" asked his aunt.

"Not good, Aunt," replied Charlie. "They discovered more damage in the basement this morning. The librarian now thinks it's deliberate so they've hired a security firm to guard the library."

"But that will cost a lot!" exclaimed McGill.

"I know," replied Charlie. "It'll use up all their money but it means that Brat Gripewater won't dare try to make any more mischief. And meanwhile who knows ... somebody somewhere might come up with the cash to save the library!"

"Let's hope so," said his aunt as Charlie walked over to the kitchen table and laid down his book.

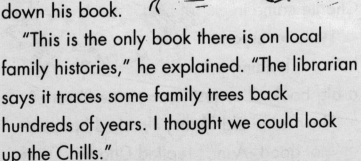

"This is the only book there is on local family histories," he explained. "The librarian says it traces some family trees back hundreds of years. I thought we could look up the Chills."

"Great," said his aunt. "Let's see. It should be very interesting."

The Chills gathered round as Charlie opened the book at the contents page. Everyone looked to see if the family name was there and Charlie pointed to it right away.

"There we are," he said, excitedly. "The Chylles!"

Bogle peered at it. "It's spelled wrong," he said.

"That must be the old-fashioned spelling of the name, Bogle," said Charlie.

"Look at this!" cried Jill as she found the chapter. "It looks like our ancestors were important people. They owned lots of land and ... a castle!" She quickly turned a page and smiled in delight. "Yes, look ... there's a plan of a castle here!"

They all stared at it and Charlie grinned, pointing to the description. "It did belong to us! To the Chylle family! Isn't that amazing? One of my ancestors might have been a baron or a duke!"

"A castle!" cried Bogle, grinning. "That means we used to be rich!" The big amiable troll began to caper round the kitchen chanting, "We used to be rich! We used to be rich!"

McGill was rapidly reading the chapter about the castle and suddenly he gasped and laughed out loud. "Ha ha!" he cried. "Guess what was built over the ruins of the old castle?"

"What?" asked Jill.

"Only the library ... and the Ghost Train!" replied McGill, chortling. "Imagine that! Our family's still in the same place after hundreds of years! And, according to this plan, the old castle had cellars. I wonder if they're still there?"

Jill shook her head in amazement. "I can't believe it," she said. "I've lived in the Ghost Train for nearly a hundred years and didn't have a clue about this!"

"Wow," breathed Charlie. "Do you think we could investigate, Aunt Jill?"

"Absolutely, Charlie," replied his aunt. "Tomorrow's Saturday, so why not come round in the morning and we'll all have a look?"

"Brilliant!" Charlie cried. "We might find something I can use in my family tree project."

"And in the meantime," said Jill, "let's try and think of something that will put a spanner in Brat's works."

Chapter Six

It was three in the morning when Lance and Slinky stopped by the side door of the darkened Ghost Train. Lance took a crowbar from a deep inside pocket and looked around him swiftly. There was not a sound to be heard or a thing to be seen. He inserted the crowbar just below the lock and heaved. The old wood splintered and as the door swung inwards a breath of cold, dank air wafted out of the darkness.

Slinky shuddered. "This place gives me the creeps."

"Don't be such a wimp," muttered Lance. "Come on." He stepped quickly into the darkness and was followed by his reluctant companion. Lance closed the door behind them and they switched on their torches.

Staring them in the face was a ghost. Its pale green body shimmered before them – hands raised and mouth open in a silent scream.

"Aaargh!" gurgled Slinky as he jerked backwards in terror.

Lance jumped with fright too before realizing there was nothing to be afraid of.

"It's only plastic!" he hissed to Slinky who was cowering behind him. "Look." He reached out and touched the ghost. The pale object floating in front of them swung gently backwards and forwards. Lance moved the beam of his torch up to the string attached to the ghost's head. "It's hanging from the ceiling!"

"Thank goodness for that," muttered Slinky, nervously shining his torch around the Ghost Train tunnel. The walls were pitted with dark crevices and it looked as if there were pairs of little eyes peering out from every nook and cranny. A large hairy thing suddenly scuttled across the roof above them and Slinky yelped in fright again.

"A spider!" he wailed.

"A spider?" muttered Lance mockingly. "You aren't afraid of spiders, are you?"

"Not usually," moaned Slinky. "But that one was as big as a football!"

"Pull yourself together," grumbled Lance, stepping on to the tracks, "and let's get going."

Following the track they crept slowly along the tunnel, with Lance counting under his breath.

"If there's a trapdoor to the old cellars it shouldn't be far ahead," he hissed. "I paced it out from the old castle wall by the library to the Ghost Train. It should only be about another ten paces or so." He shone his torch on the map and nodded. "Yeah, about another ten paces."

Slowly they moved on until Lance suddenly whispered, "Here!"

Shining the torches on the ground by their feet they began to scuff around in the dusty layer of small stones by the edge of the track. After a few minutes Slinky whispered, "There's nothing under this lot, Lance. Only old flagstones. They must have covered over the trapdoor when they built this place."

"Just keep looking," hissed Lance. "You never know what..." Suddenly he stopped and drew in his breath sharply. "Oh-ho!" he crowed softly. "What's this?"

Kneeling down he shone his torch on the object that he had uncovered with his foot.

"It's a big metal ring," muttered Slinky. "Lance, do you think that's..."

"I do, Slink," replied Lance quietly, his voice trembling with excitement. "I do! I think it's the handle of the trapdoor. Come on, give me a hand."

They pulled hard and with a creak and a groan of its rusty old hinges the trapdoor began to open slowly. A few moments later it stood stiffly upright, revealing the black opening of the secret passageway below them. A cold, earthy smell wafted out.

"This is it!" whispered Lance excitedly, shining his torch into the blackness beneath. "Come on, let's go!"

Slowly and carefully they made their way down the steps.

As they got to the bottom, their torches revealed an arched stone passageway that stretched away into the gloom. "Ah, here we are," said Lance softly. "This is definitely it!"

Slinky shuddered. "It's like the dungeons down here," he whispered.

"Probably was," Lance whispered back cheerfully. He sniggered and set off along the passageway. "A piece of cake," he gloated. "It'll be like taking candy from a baby!"

Suddenly Slinky jumped in fright.

"What's up now?" asked Lance in annoyance.

Trembling, Slinky pointed to an alcove in the passageway just ahead of them. Floating there was another pale, ghostly shape. Its hands were raised and its mouth was open in a silent cry.

Lance grinned. "You and your big imagination, Slinky," he chortled. "It's another one of those plastic ghosts. Look..." He walked forward and pushed the ghostly figure ... and his hand went right through it.

"Boo," said the ghost and began to laugh.

Lance and Slinky let out a terrified scream. "It's real!" they shrieked, their hair standing on end.

Elbowing each other aside in their desperation to get out, they stumbled and scrabbled their way back up the steps. The ghost followed them, its wild laughter ringing in their ears.

They scrambled into the Ghost Train tunnel and frantically closed the trapdoor behind them. It shut with a loud thump, but not before the ghost had escaped.

"Boo!" it cried again.

Wailing, Lance and Slinky rushed off down the tunnel with the ghost close behind, cackling insanely.

"Wooohahahahahahah!"

They wrenched open the outside door and dived through, slamming it behind them.

The ghost didn't bother to follow them. It drifted back along the passageway, its shoulders shaking, its mad laughter slowly dying away to a soft chuckle.

"Oh my," it said softly, wiping its eyes. "Oh my. I haven't had that much fun in a hundred years."

Chapter Seven

Brat was not amused when Lance and Slinky appeared at his office just before dawn, trembling and bedraggled.

"A ghost!" he snapped angrily. "You ran because you saw a ghost? What did you expect? A little bunny rabbit? It is a Ghost Train, after all! It's not real, you know. It's all make-up and special effects!"

"B-but it was real, boss," stuttered Slinky and Lance nodded in agreement.

"Rubbish!" snorted Brat.

"B-b-but…" protested Lance.

"Quiet!" cried Brat. "As usual I'll have to help you do your job." He looked disgustedly at his quivering henchmen. "We'll go to the Ghost Train right now. It's still very early and if I know those showbiz types they'll all be in their beds till noon. We'll be in and out of there with the treasure before they open their eyes."

"D-do we have to go, boss?" asked Slinky, nervously. "The treasure might not be there. And … er … aren't you rich enough anyway?"

Brat grinned greedily, gazing at his thick gold rings and puffing on his big cigar.

"You're never too rich, Slinky," he said, winking. "Never. Now, no time to lose. Let's go get that treasure!"

At 7am the Ghost Train Chills were gathered round the kitchen table, waiting for Charlie to arrive.

"Did anyone hear a funny noise in the middle of the night?" asked Jill.

"What kind of noise?" said McGill.

"Like a heavy thump," replied Jill, "followed by a strange laugh."

Thothage yawned and scratched his dusty stomach sleepily. "Probably Bogle falling out of bed," he said. "It's the kind of thing he finds funny."

"Did you fall out of bed, Bogle laddie?" asked McGill.

Bogle thought hard. "Don't think so," he replied slowly.

Before anyone could offer another suggestion the doorbell screamed … AIEEEE!

"That'll be Charlie!" cried Jill. As she made for the door a peal of wild laughter echoed weirdly down the Ghost Train tunnel.

"That wasn't Charlie!" exclaimed McGill, joining Jill at the door.

"No," replied Jill. "That was the laugh I heard in the middle of the night!" She pulled open the door quickly, hoping to see what was causing the noise. But there was only Charlie, staring off along the tunnel with a big grin on his face.

"Is that a new sound effect for the Ghost Train, Aunt?" he asked. "It's really good."

Jill shook her head. "It wasn't," she replied. "But it should be! Come on, everyone," she cried. "Let's find out what it is!"

She led the way along the narrow tracks past plastic ghosts, fake-fur monsters and waxwork witches. The tunnel turned and twisted sharply, walls glistening damply like an underground cave. Suddenly, turning a corner, they found what they were looking for. There, floating in the middle of the tunnel was a ghost. A real one. It was wearing a long nightgown and had its back to them. As they approached it turned and a huge grin split its kindly face.

"I'd know you all anywhere!" the ghost cried in delight. "You're all Chills, aren't you?!"

Charlie smiled and nodded and the Ghost Train Chills gasped with pleasure.

"Uncle Bill!" exclaimed Jill, beaming. "It's you! I recognized you right away. I've got a picture of you on the kitchen dresser. Where have you been all this time?"

They gathered round Uncle Bill excitedly and introduced themselves.

Bill said hello to each of them, his smile becoming wider and wider until suddenly he threw his head back and roared with laughter.

"Oh my!" he cried. "Oh my! It's so lovely to meet you all. I've been on my own so long that I'd quite forgotten how nice it is to have a family!"

"So where have you been all this time, Bill?" asked McGill a few minutes later when they were all back in the kitchen.

"In the cellars," replied the ghost with a grin, pointing to the floor. "Been there for a hundred years or so."

"The cellars do exist!" breathed Charlie. "Wow!"

"Incredible!" agreed Jill, shaking her head in bewilderment. "And we didn't know a thing about it." She looked at her long-lost uncle fondly. "So why haven't we seen you before now, Bill?"

"Couldn't get out," said Bill. "I'm not the kind of ghost that can walk through walls or doors, I'm afraid."

"Why were you down there?"

Bill chuckled.

"After I died I began haunting the Ghost Train. Then, one day, a workman repairing the tracks found an entrance to the cellars and opened it. I went in to have a look around. Unfortunately the workman took one look at the cellars, didn't like what he saw and promptly closed the entrance again. I got trapped. That was a hundred years ago and I've been there ever since."

"What a shame!" cried Jill. "Poor you!"

"So how did you get out, Uncle Bill?" asked Charlie.

Bill chortled. "I was let out by two silly-looking characters last night. They had come down into my cellar by the trapdoor not far from here..."

"A trapdoor!" exclaimed Charlie. "Is that the entrance you were talking about?"

"It is," replied Bill.

"Amazing!" cried Jill. "The things I don't know about my own Ghost Train! But..." she went on, frowning, "people were here ... last night? What did they look like, Bill?"

"Shifty," replied Bill. "One was thin with his hair in a pony-tail and the other was thickset with very short fair hair."

"Lance Boyle and Slinky Eels!" cried Charlie and the Chills together.

"What on earth were they doing?" said McGill.

"The thin one had a map," replied Bill, "so they were probably looking for the treasure. But I certainly scared them off." He threw back his head and laughed again. "They looked so funny as they fell over themselves trying to escape!"

"Treasure?" asked McGill disbelievingly. "You did say treasure?"

"Oh yes," replied Bill. "There's treasure all right. A box full of gold coins. Didn't you know? Belongs to our family. It's hidden at the end of the passageway. I'll show you if you like. Come on."

"Treasure!" cried Bogle happily, capering about. "We're still rich! We're still rich!"

Chapter Eight

While Bill and the Chills chatted happily in the kitchen, Lance and Slinky broke into the Ghost Train again. They crept along the tunnel, climbed through the trapdoor and hurried along the secret passageway with Brat.

"I told you there was no ghost," sneered Brat softly.

"There was one, boss, honest," protested Slinky looking round nervously. "It was in one of those dark alcoves." He shone his torch along the wall but the arched spaces were empty.

"It's probably gone to ghostie beddy-byes," said Brat mockingly. He brushed a dangling cobweb from his immaculate camel-hair coat and frowned. "This place needs a good spring clean!"

"What if someone opens the trapdoor while we're down here?" said Lance, worried. "We'll be caught red-handed."

Brat snorted. "Highly unlikely, Lance, no one knows it's there. But anyway, I'm way ahead of you. There's a bolt on this side of the trapdoor and I closed it. If someone does try to open it they'll think it's jammed shut and go away." He sniffed. "As usual I have to think of everything. Come on, no time to waste." He led the way along the passageway, checking the map as he went.

Above them in the
Ghost Train tunnel
Bogle heaved on the
iron ring of the trap
door and frowned.

"It won't open,"
he said in
surprise. "I don't want to pull
any harder or the handle will come off."

McGill whistled softly. "If you can't open it,
Bogle laddie, then no one can," he said.

"That's true," Bogle agreed sadly.

"It should open," said Bill, puzzled. "Those
two opened it easily enough last night."

"Maybe it's jammed," suggested Thothage.

"Or bolted on the inside," said Charlie
quietly.

McGill's eyes narrowed and he cracked his
bony knuckles. "You could be right, Charlie,"
he said. "Gripewater's cronies could have
come back. And there's only one way to find
out." He pointed to a narrow crack between

the edge of the trapdoor and the flagstones. "Thothage will have to go through and look."

Thothage spluttered in mid-yawn.

"Why me?" he complained.

"Because you're the only one who can transform himself into something very small," replied McGill. "Come on now, ancient Egyptian laddie. No time for hanging around."

Thothage sighed. "If I must," he muttered. "But transformations are so tiring."

He closed his eyes, stretched out his arms and chanted.

Akhenaton, Nefertiti,
Ka, Ka, Ka.
Thoth, Anubis, Ptah and Seti,
Ra, Ra, Ra!

There was a bright blue flash and a puff of green smoke and Thothage disappeared.

"He's a bat!" cried Charlie. "Look!"

The Chills looked down and saw a tiny bat on the floor at their feet.

It yawned, sighed, then disappeared into the crack between the trapdoor and the flagstones.

"Go for it, wee Thothage!" cried McGill.

"Should be around here somewhere," Brat muttered, looking at the map then swinging his torch over the dark stone walls.

"There it is, boss!" hissed Lance in excitement, indicating an ancient iron box that was lurking at the back of a small, dark alcove. His pointing finger trembled as he spoke. "It has to be the treasure!"

Thrusting his hands into the niche, Brat grabbed the box and pulled it to the edge. The box scraped heavily against the stone.

"There's definitely something in there!" he

said and pointed to the large padlock. "Do
the honours, will you, Lance?"

Lance smirked. "Glad to, boss," he said,
taking a hammer out of his pocket. He
swung it hard and the rusty padlock broke
off instantly.

Lance and Slinky peered closely as Brat
gripped the edge of the lid and pulled it open.

"Yes!" cried Brat gloatingly. "Gold coins!
This is the easiest money I've ever made!"

Suddenly Slinky jumped and flapped his
hand at something in the air.

"It's a bat!" he yelped. "I don't like bats!"

The little bat fluttered round their heads
then flew off back down the passageway.

Brat sneered, "Don't be such a scaredy-cat, Slinky." He grabbed the box and held it

tightly. "Time to go!" he crowed. "We've got what we came for!" He set off along the passageway, his two cronies following closely. They hadn't  gone far when Brat stopped and listened.

"What's up?" asked Lance nervously.

Brat frowned suspiciously. "I heard a noise coming from the direction of the trapdoor," he muttered.

"Do you think maybe there's someone there?" hissed Slinky fearfully.

"Better not to take any chances," replied Brat and turned back the way he had come. "Come on, follow me. I went over the map again yesterday and I reckon I discovered another way out!"

Chapter Nine

The Chills were gathered round the trapdoor as the little bat reappeared.

A moment later there was a bright blue flash, a cloud of yellow smoke and Thothage stood there once more.

He stretched and gave a huge yawn. "I'm ready for bed now," he said.

"What did you see?" asked McGill urgently. "Is anyone down there?"

Thothage nodded sleepily. "Brat and his two cronies. And they've found the treasure."

Jill grinned. "Well," she said, "it won't do them any good. They're trapped. All we have to do is wait here till they come out. Then we'll retrieve the treasure."

Bill began to look worried. "I wonder..." he muttered and stared down the tunnel. "You stay here," he said suddenly to the others. "I'm going to check something." And without a backward glance he swooped away around the corner.

"What's he up to?" said McGill, scratching his bony head.

"I'll go and find out, Great Grandpa," replied Charlie, dashing after the ghost.

👣 👣 👣

"Aha!" crowed Brat. "I was right!" He and his two nervous henchmen were standing at the top of a narrow flight of steps and above them was another wooden trapdoor. "This should take us out at the other side of the Ghost Train," he said smugly, hurrying up the steps. "Am I a genius or what?"

"You're a genius," replied Lance admiringly.

With some effort he and Lance pushed open the trapdoor. Its covering of small stones and thick dust slid off on to the track making a dull rattling sound. Nervously Lance peered out.

"We're still in the Ghost Train," he hissed, "but I can see a door marked exit. There's no one about."

"Excellent," murmured Brat. "Let's get out of here and count that money!"

They clambered out of the trapdoor and closed it quietly behind them. But just as they were about to head for the door a wild, unearthly howl made them freeze in their tracks. They spun round and came face to face with Bill. He hovered in the air, an icy look on his ghostly face.

"My treasure," he hissed fiercely. "Give me back my treasure!"

Lance and Slinky wailed in terror and turned and fled through the door. Brat backed off slowly, his eyes narrowed suspiciously, the box still clutched tightly to his chest.

"You're not real!" he muttered hoarsely. "It's all a trick."

At that moment Charlie came round the corner and stopped. Right away he saw that Brat would not let go of the box and that Bill probably couldn't take it from him. Brat hadn't spotted him yet, so Charlie quickly seized the head from a nearby plastic monster and pulled it on. Then, letting out the loudest shriek he could muster, he ran at Brat.

Brat's head snapped round and his eyes glazed over as he saw a small, screaming green and red monster running at him. He turned and stumbled towards the door. Just as he got there, however, the Ghost Train Chills came running round the opposite corner.

Jill spotted Brat with the box and realized immediately that it was the treasure. She stopped and, flinging out her arms, let out her special operatic scream.

"AAAAAAAAAAAAAAEEEEEEEEEEEEEEEE OOOOOOOOOO!"

Brat froze as the awful sound blasted past him.

Then Bogle, Thothage and McGill, taking their cue from Jill, did likewise. Arms outstretched, they all began to walk slowly towards Brat, screaming like banshees. The howling, terrifying screech of the Ghost Train Chills bounced off the walls of the tunnel, making Brat's hair stand on end and his eyes pop. He stood, transfixed in horror as the horrible, screaming creatures slowly advanced towards him, their bony hands reaching, reaching...

"It's not real," he whimpered in disbelief, one hand on the doorknob, the other still clutching the treasure.
"It can't be real!"

Before he knew what was happening the
little monster ran up to him, snatched the
box from his
grasp and
ran off
round the
corner.

The ghost threw its head back and his howl
of laughter joined the screams of the Chills in
a mad, rising cacophony of sound. Brat was
shaken to his boots. He couldn't take any
more. His ears hurt and he couldn't believe
his eyes. He'd had enough of Ghost Trains
and haunted treasure to last him a long, long
time. Turning, he wrestled the door open and
ran out into the rainy car park.

The screams of the Ghost Train Chills turned
into laughter as the door slammed and Charlie
came back round the corner with the box.

"We did it," said Bogle happily. "We saved
the treasure!"

"I arrived just in time," said Bill, wiping the tears of laughter from his eyes. "You should've seen their faces!"

"But how did you know Brat and his cronies would be here, Bill?" asked Jill.

"I didn't," replied Bill. "I just suddenly remembered there was another trapdoor and wondered if they'd use that to get out."

"It's lucky you were around, Bill," remarked McGill, smiling.

"And now that you're here you'll stay," Jill said fondly. "Won't you, Bill?"

Bill laughed. "I certainly will," he replied. "But only if I can join you all working in the Ghost Train."

"Brilliant!" cried the Chills. "A real live ghost is just what we need!"

"We could even put railway tracks in the cellars!" exclaimed McGill. "Have a two-tier Ghost Train!"

"And there's a job for you here if you want it, Charlie," said his aunt with a broad grin.

"That was a wonderful bit of scaring you did!"

"I don't think Mum and Dad would be too keen on that suggestion!" said Charlie, grinning.

"What about the treasure?" asked Bogle, tossing the heavy box from hand to hand as if it were a box of tissues. "Now that we've got it I don't really want to be rich. I like things the way they are."

"Me too," said Jill and McGill, and Thothage nodded in agreement.

"We could use it to save the library," said Charlie quietly. "That would be a good use of the money, wouldn't it?"

Everyone turned to Charlie in delight.

"Of course!" cried his aunt, beaming. "The library! Perfect! What a wonderful idea, Charlie!"

"And it's divine justice for Brat," said Charlie. "Just think. We wouldn't have found out about the treasure if it hadn't been for him. So in a weird way we've got him to thank for saving the library!"

"He won't be very pleased when he realizes that," said Jill. "But it serves him right."

"It certainly does, Aunt Jill," replied Charlie with a big grin. "He really should know better than to meddle with the Chills!"